HOPE

Stories for a Healthy Mind

Published by Scholastic India Pvt. Ltd.
A subsidiary of Scholastic Inc., New York, 10012 (USA).
Publishers since 1920, with international operations in Canada, Australia, New Zealand, the United Kingdom, India, and Hong Kong.

For information regarding permission, write to:
Scholastic India Pvt. Ltd.
A-27, Ground Floor, Sigma Centre
Infocity-1, Sector 34, Gurgaon-122001 (India)

First edition: September 2020
Reprint: January 2021, February 2021, October 2022, December 2022, November 2024

ISBN-13: 978-93-90189-18-2

Printed in India at Sai Printo Pack Pvt Ltd, New Delhi

Hope

Stories for a Healthy Mind

Written by
Pragati Sureka

Illustrated by
Nina Sud

SCHOLASTIC
New York Toronto London Auckland
Sydney New Delhi Hong Kong

A MESSAGE FROM SCHOLASTIC INDIA

The stories in this book aren't just 'stories'. Our protagonists Ryan, Kabir and Shoma are each faced with a unique situation, whether its domestic unrest, depression or compulsive behaviour. These are all realities that we need to talk about and address.

As a parent, this book is absolutely essential. We all want our children to be raised with healthy and happy minds and this is a good place to start.

Shantanu Duttagupta
Publisher

RYAN

The school bell rang out loud and clear.

All the children rushed towards the assembly hall. Most of the kids walked with their friends, some in big groups, others in pairs. One or two children walked alone quietly. They wished they were a part of those groups, where the kids were pushing each other, whispering and giggling together.

In a quiet classroom, Ryan was sitting at his desk. He hadn't heard the bell. He seemed to be in another world. He was lost in his thoughts.

His friend Avi had heard the bell. He quickly poked Ryan in his arm and raced past him. This was just like Avi! He was always in a rush, always moving fast. No wonder Avi won in the races held on Sports Day.

Ryan gave Avi a glare and slowly stood up. Avi and his best friend, Kabir, were waiting for him near the door. When the bell rang again, and Ryan still didn't hurry, Avi pulled Kabir's hand and the two boys ran to the assembly hall.

Ryan didn't like being left alone. He didn't want to attend the assembly either. He dragged his feet towards the hall. Naturally, he was late. By the time Ryan found his seat, the assembly was about to start.

Mrs Rai, their class teacher, frowned at him.

Shoma nudged Radha. They both knew that Ryan would get scolded after the assembly, yet again.

Radha whispered, 'Slow-poke!' in Shoma's ear and both the girls started giggling.

But Ryan did not notice any of this as he was lost in thought again. He kept remembering the big fight that had happened between his mummy and papa last night. Their angry words and screams kept going round and round in his head.

He had hidden at the top of the stairs and watched the fight. Neither Mummy nor Papa had seen him. They had told him to go to his room. He had tried to sleep. But when they started shouting at each other, even his favourite dinosaur pillow couldn't muffle the noise. So he went and sat on the steps to make sure they didn't hurt each other.

He felt so scared and angry and so very alone.

Was it because of me? He kept thinking. Are they fighting because they think I am a bad boy? Maybe it was because I got scolded in class again, or forgot to put my toys back.

How he prayed to God to make him a good boy. He wanted his mummy and papa to be happy and always be laughing and smiling like Avi's mummy and daddy. Nobody shouted and screamed in Avi's house. They just hugged and kissed him and his little brother Rohan all the time.

Sometimes, Avi would forget to put back his toys. His mummy scolded him but she and his daddy never looked angry and screamed at each other like his mummy and papa. Maybe Avi was a much better boy than him. Maybe if he could become more like Avi, then his mummy and papa would be happy and they could all live happily.

Mrs Rai saw the sad look on Ryan's face. She noticed that all the children were laughing during the puppet show at the assembly. All the children, except Ryan. He was upset about something and hadn't paid any attention at all. Later, when all the children had gone back to class, Mrs Rai asked Ryan to see her in the staffroom during break time.

Ryan knocked on the staffroom door some hours later. Mrs Rai smiled at him kindly and told him to come in. She noticed that although his chin was lifted up, his eyes looked troubled and sad.

On an impulse, she gave him a warm hug. Ryan was not used to such kindness. Immediately, his tears started to fall. Mrs Rai took him aside to a quiet corner and made him sit down next to her. She took out a handkerchief and wiped his face gently. Then she gave him a cookie and said, 'What is bothering you, Ryan? Please tell me what's wrong.'

Slowly, between bites of the sweet chocolate chip cookie, the truth came out. Ryan told his teacher about the ugly fights between Mummy and Papa. He told her about how ashamed and guilty he felt. 'It's because of me,' he said, sadly. 'I'm the one who makes them angry. It's all my fault.'

Mrs Rai shook her head and hugged Ryan again. 'That's not true, Ryan,' she said kindly. 'You are a good, sweet boy. Your mummy and papa must be angry because of something else.'

'Then why do they keep their fights a secret from me? No one tells me anything!' Ryan said angrily.

He told her about all his angry thoughts. Mrs Rai heard him out patiently.

'I feel lonely and upset. My parents don't talk to me when they fight,' he said. 'I wish God would make me better. But no matter how hard I try, the fights and shouting just doesn't stop.'

Mrs Rai hugged him tightly again. 'I'll speak to your parents about this, Ryan. No, don't worry. I won't scold them.' She smiled. Ryan broke into a small smile at the little joke. The ugly tight feeling in his chest had lessened. 'Now, finish your cookie and go play with your friends. Everything will be all right.'

The next day, Mrs Rai called Ryan's parents to school. She spoke to them after class was over. Ryan waited outside impatiently. He couldn't hear what they were saying because the door was shut. Would Mummy and Papa be angry with him? Would they start fighting again? He wondered.

Inside the classroom, his mother and father were talking to Mrs Rai. They were shocked to learn about how Ryan had been feeling. His mother started crying when she heard that Ryan blamed himself. His father shook his head sadly.

Mrs Rai said, 'I know how hard all this must be for you and Ryan. It might be a good idea to seek help from a family therapist or counsellor.'

'Yes, that is a good idea,' said Ryan's mother.

'I agree. It would be good to talk to a doctor to help to sort out these issues,' said Ryan's father.

By this time, Ryan was very worried. He peeped inside the classroom through the window. He looked at his parents and Mrs Rai trying to guess the mood. The teacher spotted his worried face and called him in.

Putting her arm around him, she smiled and said, 'Don't worry, Ryan. I told you everything was going to be okay. Your mummy and papa love you very much.'

Then she carefully explained, 'Sometimes, when people are upset about something else, they get angry with each other. It doesn't mean that you are to blame. Your mummy and papa are dealing with some big people problems. They are going to take help from a relationship expert.'

'Ex-expert?' Ryan asked, his chin wobbling from holding back tears.

'A relationship expert is a specially trained person,' said Mrs Rai, 'who can help us talk to each other about our feelings. They can help solve problems that sometimes happen between two people.'

'Like a doctor for feelings?' Ryan asked, wide-eyed.

'Something like that,' replied Mrs Rai, smiling. 'Now, I think your parents want to tell you something.' She gently pushed him towards them.

As soon as he came around the teacher's desk, Ryan's mummy pulled him into a bear hug. His papa stood up and walked around his mummy's chair. He crouched down next to Ryan and rubbed his back. Mrs Rai left the room so that they could talk to each other privately.

'We're so sorry, Ryan,' said Mummy, her eyes filled with tears. 'Sometimes Mummy and Papa fight and it can be scary. We promise not to shout at each other anymore.'

'We love you so much, Ryan,' Daddy said in his deep rumbling voice. 'We're not angry with you. Please don't think we blame you for anything. You are the most important person in our lives!'

Mummy and Papa hugged Ryan tightly. He felt a lot better. That horrible ouchy feeling had gone from his chest. He just felt warm and happy now. Mrs Rai was right: Everything was going to be okay.

His parents thanked Mrs Rai for her help. Then they gave Ryan another tight hug and left. Ryan waved goodbye to them as they crossed the school grounds. Mrs Rai stood next to him, smiling, her arm around Ryan's shoulders.

Ryan smiled back at her. The school bell rang. The next period had begun! He went back to his desk, whistling and smiling.

KABIR

One evening, Kabir and his mummy were making dinner together in the kitchen.

They were cutting vegetables to put in the soup. Kabir liked helping his mummy in the kitchen. They would talk, crack jokes, laugh—being with Mummy was so much fun.

Dad, on the other hand, well, Kabir wasn't sure Dad liked him very much nowadays. He was always so angry with him. And when he wasn't angry, he just didn't care what Kabir was doing.

Kabir was tired of wondering why Dad kept getting mad at him. So he'd decided to ask Mummy once and for all.

'Have I done something wrong again?' Kabir said. 'Dad looks so angry today. I think he hates me.'

Mummy stopped chopping carrots and turned towards Kabir, shocked. 'Why would you think that, Kabir? That's not true. Your dad loves you very, very much.'

Kabir shook his head. 'No, Mummy, I don't think so. He's always angry with me. Yesterday, he scolded me because I was laughing too loudly while watching cartoons. He ...' Kabir hesitated and looked at Mummy, wondering whether he should go on.

When Mummy nodded, Kabir let out a sigh of relief. Mummy wasn't mad at him! Suddenly, all the sad, upset feelings that been clogged up inside him burst out. Kabir told Mummy everything.

'Last week,' Kabir began, fidgeting with a napkin, 'Dad smacked me because I did not finish the food on my plate. I tried to tell him I had had a big glass of milk in the evening and was feeling too full. But he didn't listen. I fell down and the plate slipped from my hand. Dina and I cleaned it up before you saw.'

'Oh, Kabir, why didn't you tell me?' Mummy cried out, gathering Kabir close to her. 'I would have scolded Dad.'

'No!' said Kabir. 'Dad would have yelled at you then. He always yells at you. I hate it! I hate him!' Angry tears spilled down Kabir's cheeks.

'Hush, Kabir! You mustn't say that—' Mummy said.

'It's true! Today morning, during breakfast, when I said the toast was burned and tasted funny, he yelled at me to "Shut up!" And then, when Dina and I were joking with each other in the car on the way to school, he yelled at us again. Why does he keep yelling, Mummy? Dina got so scared, she started crying.'

'I'm so sorry, Kabir,' said Mummy, wiping away Kabir's tears. 'It's not your fault or Dina's. It's not even Dad's fault. Dad isn't well, Kabir.'

'He's sick?' Kabir asked, surprised. 'He doesn't look sick. He doesn't cough or sneeze like Dina and me when we catch a cold or the flu.'

'Dad's illness is a bit different,' said Mummy. 'You are a big boy now so I think you'll be able to understand what I'm about to tell you. Dad has an illness called "Depression".'

'Wh-what happens during depression?' asked Kabir, feeling worried about his dad. He also felt guilty and ashamed for saying he hated him.

'Well, there are different types of depression,' Mummy explained. 'In your dad's case, he rarely feels calm and has trouble relaxing or being patient. He also gets angry at the drop of a hat. You know the feeling when you're having a bad day and everything makes you angry and grumpy?'

Kabir nodded.

'Yes, well, Dad feels the same. The only difference is that Dad feels like that every day,' Mummy said.

'How did it happen?' Kabir asked, taking the carrot Mummy was offering him and munching on it.

'Dad's work is very stressful. You know how he hates to talk about his feelings.' Kabir nodded again. His dad would always try and hide whenever he was sad or upset. In fact, until recently, he never really used to show his anger either. This was also why Kabir was so upset—he had never seen his dad behave like this.

'After a while,' continued Mummy, 'Dad started feeling very upset because of the stress. His inner being slowly became very uncomfortable and his thoughts about himself and others became negative. His behaviour became like two ends of a see-saw.'

Kabir frowned. He didn't like see-saws very much. They were always moving up and down. He always felt like he was going to fall off and hurt himself. He liked the sturdiness of the jungle gym instead. It was steady and never moved or threw him off-balance.

'Is that why his mood goes up and down too? How difficult for Dad!' Kabir cried.

'It can be,' Mummy agreed. 'And very tiring too. Sometimes, he is extremely angry and irritable. At other times, he is very sad and does not want to do anything or talk to anyone.

'At first, like Dina and you, Dad and I couldn't understand what was happening. Then our doctor told us to go to a psychiatrist—an expert who helps

Dr. Tara Mishra

people understand how their mind works and how to control their inner being,' she explained, when she saw the confused look on Kabir's face.

'Oh, I get it now,' Kabir said. Mummy smiled and ruffled his hair.

'The expert told us the importance of having a healthy mind. Just like we need to take care of our body, we also need to take care of our mind. This includes our thoughts and feelings.'

'How can we do that, Mummy? What will make Dad feel better?' asked Kabir.

'Don't worry, Kabir,' said Mummy, as she put the chopped vegetables in a pot. 'The doctor made Dad and me understand how to cope with Dad's mood swings. The psychiatrist also gave Dad medicine after doing some blood tests. These will help him feel better and calmer.'

'So he won't yell at us anymore?' Kabir asked hopefully.

'He'll try very hard not to. But remember, we need to help Daddy as well,' Mummy replied as she stirred the pot. 'Depression requires time to get better. Daddy needs to go to the doctor regularly so he can share his feelings and thoughts in a safe space.'

'Is that like what I'm doing here? Telling you how I feel?' Kabir asked Mummy.

'It's similar,' said Mummy. 'But not exactly the same. Dad's problems need a properly trained expert. Someone who can teach him how to deal with his stress and anger.'

'How can I help him, Mummy?' Kabir asked eagerly. 'What can I do?'

Mummy kissed Kabir on his forehead. 'You're such a good boy! You and Dina just need to be a little patient with Dad. Remember, he has just started taking his medicine and going to the doctor. It takes time to start getting better. But you can come and talk to me whenever you feel upset. Most importantly, you must always remember that Dad loves you very, very much. So, what say, champ? Do we have a deal?' Mummy held out her hand for Kabir to shake.

Kabir shook it solemnly. He replied, his big brown eyes very serious, 'I'll do my best to help Dad. I don't hate him, you know? Not really. I was just so upset because he kept yelling at us. Now I understand how difficult it is for him. He'll get better, won't he?'

'Yes, he will.' Mummy smiled. 'Now come and help me lay the table.'

'Sure,' Kabir replied, climbing off the stool he'd been sitting on. Before he left the kitchen, he ran to his mummy and gave her a big hug!

'What's this for?' said Mummy, laughing.

Kabir smiled, 'Thank you for explaining everything to me. I was scared you'd tell me it wasn't important.'

'Oh, Kabir, no,' Mummy replied, hugging Kabir back. 'Talking about your feelings is very important.

Otherwise, they build up inside you and erupt like a volcano, hurting both you and the people around you as well. If you can't talk about it, how will you fix it?'

'Just like Dad is getting his problems fixed?' Kabir asked.

'Yes, just like Dad is getting help. You're very brave—just like your Dad!' Mummy smiled and then nudged Kabir towards the door. 'Now go and call everyone for dinner! Or else it'll get cold and then I will yell at all of you!'

Kabir laughed and raced out of the room. He and Dina would do their best to help Dad feel better. Maybe, soon there won't be any yelling in the house. Soon, there would be laughter instead.

SHOMA

'It's time to sleep, Shoma!' Mummy called out from the living room.

Shoma looked at the wall clock and then at her bookshelf. She gave a sigh of relief. Finally, all the books were stacked neatly, in alphabetical order and according to size. It had only taken her two hours this time. She was getting faster, Shoma smiled to herself, before letting out a big yawn.

It was ten-thirty at night and her eyes were droopy with sleep. But she couldn't help looking over her room one more time. Her mind was still active; in fact, it was overactive. Suddenly, she spotted something.

She nibbled on her thumbnail as she walked to her desk. The pencils were mixed up in the pencil

stand. Had her sister, Raina, or their brother Shiv, taken something from her desk again? What else had they messed up? Oh, she hated it when they took something from her room and didn't put it back in its place.

Now she could not go to bed till her desk looked perfectly neat. It was as though she was glued to her chair. She would only get up once she had arranged her desk properly.

Sighing, she emptied the pencil stand onto her desk. Then, carefully, she put back the six pencils in the stand. She spent five minutes arranging them so that none of the pencils were sticking out oddly. If they weren't arranged properly, Shoma thought, she would get that tight achy feeling in her chest again. She felt her heart start to pound as the thought slipped into her mind.

Clutter in any form was not okay with her. It made her upset and restless. Why couldn't anyone else understand that everything had to kept in its

proper place or be done at a fixed time? Everyone talked about neatness, but no one seemed to really practice it. Instead, they all teased her whenever she would get upset that her books had been moved or when her siblings had taken something from her room and not put it back in its proper place.

Finally, the pencils were in perfect order, the clips and erasers placed neatly in a little box, the school books stacked in a straight line.

And then a thought made her pale. What if Shiv or Raina had moved her pencil box as well? What if they had misplaced her school books for tomorrow? What if she went to school and opened her bag, only to discover that something was missing? Oh no!

Shoma felt terribly worried ... and tired. Her mind was always thinking of a thousand things that could go wrong. It was hard to think about anything else when she felt worried like this.

Just to make sure, she repacked her school bag as well. The pencil box was always kept in front, followed by two notebooks and two bigger books. There was a soft face napkin folded thrice into a little square—this was in its place in the front pocket. Mummy would put the water bottle in the outer pocket on the right. Her

dinosaur lunch box was kept in the frontmost pocket. Shoma carefully leaned the bag against the side of the desk and shifted it about till it was in the perfect position. She stepped back and looked at it again and then shifted it a little to the side. There—now it was all right.

Once she finished, she went to her bed and was about to get in, when she stopped. Frowning, she tidied the soft blue bedsheet, removing the wrinkle she had spotted. Then, she fluffed her pillows, arranged her three bolsters in a row—first the yellow one, then the one with the pink flowers and finally, the blue and white polka-dotted one. Next, she lay down and rearranged her floral duvet around her till it reached midway up her chest. Finally, at 11:30 p.m., when she was satisfied, she allowed herself to go to sleep, snuggling up to Mr Teddy. This wasn't unusual for Shoma—however neatly her bed was made, she always needed to remake it. She could not help it.

Next morning, the shrill sound of the alarm woke her up. Shoma turned off the alarm, carefully putting it back in its place. Then she quickly folded back the duvet, making sure that the sides of the duvet lined up exactly with the edges of the mattress. She smoothened the sheets, put her pillows back in order and only then did she allow herself to go to the bathroom to get ready for school.

Unfortunately, this meant she was late to the breakfast table. 'Late again, sleepyhead!' Shiv and Raina called out over their shoulders as they raced out of the front door towards the bus stop. Unlike her, they had already finished breakfast. Now, the school bus was already here and Shoma would miss it … again.

She hung her head down in shame.

Her mother saw her expression and gave her a hug. She understood the reason for her daughter's unhappiness. She didn't ruffle her hair because she knew that would only upset Shoma further. Instead, she rubbed Shoma's shoulder soothingly and said, 'Don't worry, darling. Papa will drop you to school in his car. Everyone gets a little late sometimes. Now, finish your toast, milk and banana.'

Shoma looked at her gratefully. 'Thanks, Mummy.' She smiled. Thank God, Mummy was not like Radhika's mother who scolded her for every little thing. Radhika had told her that she never felt she could do anything right. Shoma's mummy always let her be and didn't tease her like everyone else—

'Stop wool-gathering, Shoma!' Dadi's sharp voice pulled her from her thoughts.

She frowned into her milk. Why does Dadi never seem happy with her? Dadi was forever 'explaining' things to Shoma but she could never understand anything Dadi said. This was probably because Dadi's sharp words cut like a knife and hurt her. Shoma would feel upset and angry and not want to do anything Dadi asked her to.

There wasn't any point in telling Dadi how she felt, however. She always got angry and told Shoma, 'I am saying it for your own good!' She just didn't realize how difficult it was for Shoma to hear Dadi's 'corrections' all the time.

'Come on, Shoma. Let's go to school. I'll put on the radio channel you like.' A gentle hand stroked Shoma's back. Shoma looked up at her father. Papa was smiling at her. He laughed as he saw the neat bites she had taken of her peanut-buttered toast.

Shoma didn't mind. Like Mummy, Papa never teased her or became impatient with her. He understood she needed to do things in her own way. Otherwise, she would start feeling that everything was wrong and something terrible was going to happen. Shoma put her spoon in the exact centre of her plate when she finished and wiped all the crumbs away from her clothes. She did this slowly and carefully, ignoring Dadi's sharp comment about being late for school.

So busy was she with her little task that she didn't see the look her parents shared. They knew that Shoma was forever feeling worried and upset if things weren't exactly as she wanted them. They were also aware of how she could not do anything else till she had 'fixed' whatever was bothering her, whether it was removing wrinkles from clothes or counting her textbooks. They knew the time had come to seek help from a counsellor or clinical psychologist to deal with the situation. Shoma needed help and there was nothing wrong about it. Mummy and Papa were going to make sure that Shoma could learn to handle what was bothering her.

Later that day, they went to Mrs Dheer, a gentle and well-known child psychologist who guided them on how to approach Shoma. She heard them out patiently. Then, she asked them to come with Shoma the following week.

That evening, Shoma was called to her parents' room. 'Is everything all right?' Shoma asked, worried. Her parents never called her alone to their room like this. 'Have I done something wrong?'

'My darling Shoma!' her mother said, putting a comforting arm around her. 'You've done nothing wrong. It's just that for the last few months, Dad and I have noticed that you seem very troubled. You are always tired and cranky. No, I'm not scolding you, darling,' her mother said quickly when she saw Shoma's face crumple. 'We're just worried about you. We want you to know that you can talk to us about anything. Is there something bothering you?'

Perhaps it was the gentle way they asked or the concern on their faces, Shoma couldn't help herself. She felt as if all her worries and upsetting thoughts were rushing out of her. She tearfully shared how she could not stop herself from doing her rituals even when she knew she was going to be late. She talked about how upset she got if things weren't exactly so and the horrible heavy feeling in her chest if she didn't 'fix' what was wrong.

When she was finished, Mummy and Papa hugged her tightly. 'We're very proud of you for telling us,' said Papa. Mummy nodded. Shoma felt much, much better. No one had made fun of her or scolded her for 'being silly' as Dadi called it.

'We are going to help you sort this out, Shoma,' Mummy said. 'Mrs Dheer is a psychologist who is going to show you how to overcome these things. Does that sound all right to you?'

Shoma nodded, a little worried. However, when Papa said, 'Don't worry, we'll be right there with you, darling,' Shoma felt much better.

The following week, Mrs Dheer started her sessions with Shoma and her parents. Mrs Dheer was

patient and kind and helped explain to Shoma why she acted the way she did.

Slowly, over the next few months, with the help of Mrs Dheer and the support of everyone in Shoma's family, even Dadi, Shoma's compulsive behaviours lessened and were finally under control. Shoma wasn't late for school anymore and managed to catch the school bus with Shiv and Raina. Sometimes, she even managed to reach the bus stop before them!

Shoma and her whole family were happier than ever—all because Shoma had been a brave girl and taken help to sort out what was bothering her.

NOTE FOR PARENTS

While IQ, basic verbal and numerical abilities are stressed on in the current academic scenario, the impact of feelings is largely ignored. An awareness of basic concepts regarding EQ or emotional quotient and the ability to handle thoughts and feelings which result in healthy behaviour is beneficial for both parents and children. This understanding helps young children develop holistically into healthy, happy adults.

The three stories you read will help you and your children identify feelings and learn to regulate them for proactive social behaviour.

Children will also learn how to deal with common issues—either by self-help or learning to seek help when needed.

This will serve as a preventive measure in curtailing dysfunctional patterns which often carry down from generation to generation if not handled appropriately. The core themes of the three stories are further explained below.

RYAN

This story deals with behaviourial issues at school due to conflict between parents. Often children perform poorly in school or are distracted due to unnecessary worries. When they see or hear conflict at home, in order to cope up with the resultant insecurities and fears, they tend to wrongly blame themselves. This in turn leads to behavioural issues in the child.

Good communication, harmony at home, peaceful communication patterns, loving gestures and warm hugs go a long way in fostering a happy and alert mind in children.

KABIR

Depression is a kind of mood disorder which has become prevalent in many families today. It is commonly characterized by feeling low, inactive, lack of appetite, yelling, lack of emotional control, mood swings, irritability, sleep disturbances, loss of interest in work and fun, anger and negative thoughts. Unfortunately, there is a lot of stigma and secrecy attached to mental health issues. Such issues are often not explained to children, and because they do not understand what is going on, they get adversely affected.

Just like in this story, a simple explanation of the disease and its impact on the family eases the child's discomfort and helps him adapt to the situation in a healthy manner.

SHOMA

The third story looks at Obsessive Compulsive Disorder. In children, it is present when they have repetitive compulsive anxiety filled thoughts which hamper their routine activities. They feel a lot of tension and engage in repetitive actions which they are unable to control. Parents and family members usually get irritated by these behaviours and reprimand them which spells disaster for their mental health. Criticism by significant family members and care givers as well as genetic factors usually cause it to develop.

Successful treatment includes seeking help from a psychologist, trained in CBT preferably, who can help the child control and manage these intrusive thoughts. Parents are also guided on helpful behaviour which include providing a loving and supportive environment at home with no criticism, and good communication among family members. The chances of recovery are good with timely intervention.

While neatness is a good habit for children to learn, it needs to be differentiated from obsessive compulsive behaviours. Early detection and timely management lead to good prognosis.

Most problems in children's behaviours result from low self-esteem and unnecessary criticism that they are subjected to. To raise emotionally intelligent children, good communication patterns and harmony at home are essential. Children are highly resilient. When dysfunctional patterns of communication between adults around them or with them is checked, they bounce back very quickly. Most of their behavioural challenges disappear and they learn healthy patterns from a young age which in turn become lifelong habits and sound personal resources. They grow up as happier children who become mentally sound and healthy adults.

Here are some key practices to enhance self-esteem in your children

Be a role model

Parents need to treat children with honesty and courtesy if they expect them to learn these values.

Help them become independent

When kids make their own age-appropriate choices, they learn to face the consequences of their decisions. Thus, they become responsible.

Demonstrate affection by lovingly touching them, hugging them, smiling at them

Children understand affectionate, caring touch. So build it consciously into your body language and interpersonal exchanges.

Crack jokes with them

Humour is a potent tool for developing social skills and fostering the foundation of strong interpersonal relations.

Be loving towards your spouse

Nothing makes a child's world as secure as a set of parents who share camaraderie and mutual love and affection for each other.

Respond instead of reacting

Parents need to respond to situations with emotional stability instead of reacting, to help children develop emotional intelligence.

What you should take care to avoid

Don't take decisions for your children

Let children meet small challenges independently to master life skills. The more they meet new challenges, the more competent and confident they will feel.

Don't compare

Comparison is the first step to destroying self-esteem; it's a very negative act.

Don't criticize or taunt children

Sometimes, parents unknowingly laugh at a child's friend, choice of dress or friend, and so on, which does untold damage to a child's self-esteem.

Don't do everything for them

Be understanding, supportive and patient, and let them work things out for themselves. This way they learn responsibility, which is a lifelong asset that helps them develop their personality.

Don't bully

It makes them vulnerable to being bullied, or they bully other weaker children at school, just to take out the irritation or anger that they feel towards their parents.

ACKNOWLEDGEMENTS

I would like to thank my spouse, Sumit Sureka, for inspiring me to pen down my thoughts and helping me grow.

I would like to thank my children, Abhyuday and Nandini, for being the wind beneath my wings and for constantly motivating me to be a good role model for them.

I would like to thank my parents, my in-laws, Jyoti, Stuti and Aryana for being supportive always and motivating me to tap my potential.

ABOUT THE AUTHOR

Pragati Jalan Sureka has been working in the field of mental health for over fifteen years. Besides her dual qualifications in Clinical and Occupational Health Psychology, she has professional credentials from Harvard Medical School, Boston; The Psychometric Centre at The University of Cambridge, UK and Beck Institute, Philadelphia. Her guiding philosophy is that 'emotional well-being' is possible for everyone.

She regularly conducts workshops on mental health and emotional well-being. She is currently pursuing her Phd and is also a faculty member at Kornash, The Lifestyle Management School, Kolkata, which is a mental health vocational training facility. *Hope: Stories for a Healthy Mind* is her second book.